P9-CQQ-102

Counting in

the Garden

Kim Parker

Orchard Books ❀ New York
An Imprint of Scholastic Inc.

All rights reserved. Published by Orchard Books, an imprint of Scholastic Inc.

ORCHARD BOOKS and design are registered trademarks of Watts Publishing Group, Ltd., used under license.

SCHOLASTIC and associated logos are trademarks and/or registered trademarks of Scholastic Inc.

Library of Congress Cataloging-in-Publication Data

Parker, Kim.   Counting in the garden / Kim Parker.–1st ed.   p. cm.

Summary: Invites the reader to count the inhabitants of a garden, from one to ten, such as four bunnies and nine inchworms.

ISBN 0-439-69452-3   [1. Animals–Fiction. 2. Gardens–Fiction. 3. Counting.] I. Title. PZ7.P2265Co 2005

[E]–dc22 2004009081   10 9 8 7 6 5 4   07 08 09

Printed in Mexico 49 Reinforced Binding for Library Use First edition, April 2005

The text type was set in 36-point P22 Garamouche.

The illustrations in this book were painted in watercolor.

Book design by Alison Klapthor

To Felipe and Maggie,
two creatures I always count on.

1 cat

purring in the garden.

2 turtles

meeting in the leaves.

3 dogs

frolicking in the posies.

 bunnies

finding love in the shade.

5 dragonflies

darting between the daisies.

6 ladybugs

tiptoeing along a stem.

 birds

nesting among the blossoms.

 **bumblebees**

buzzing in the blooms.

9 inchworms

inching toward the petals.

10 butterflies

flitting among the flowers.

1 2

Counting in the
garden

4
3 5

6 8 7

from
ONE to TEN!

9 10

BATMAN'S
DARK SECRET

BY KELLEY PUCKETT

ILLUSTRATED BY JON J MUTH

BATMAN CREATED BY BOB KANE

SCHOLASTIC PRESS · NEW YORK

TO NATALIE, NICOLE, CHRISTOPHER, AND AUSTIN — KP

TO NIKOLAI — JJM

BOB KANE created the character of Batman, which was first seen in *Detective Comics #27* (May 1939). Batman has been called the Caped Crusader, the Dark Knight, and the World's Greatest Detective. Batman does not have any superpowers. Rather, he fights crime with the help of his intelligence, physical strength, wealth, martial arts, and technology.

LIBRARY OF CONGRESS CATALOGING-IN-PUBLICATION DATA
Puckett, Kelley, author.
Batman's dark secret / by Kelley Puckett ; illustrated by Jon J Muth ; Batman created by Bob Kane. — First hardcover edition.   pages cm
Originally published in 1999.
Summary: The orphan boy Bruce Wayne conquers his fear of the dark, making it possible for him to grow up and become the crime-fighting hero Batman.
ISBN 978-0-545-86755-9
1. Batman (Fictitious character)—Juvenile fiction. 2. Fear of the dark—Juvenile fiction.
3. Orphans—Juvenile fiction. 4. Heroes—Juvenile fiction. [1. Fear of the dark—Fiction. 2. Orphans—Fiction. 3. Superheroes—Fiction.] I. Muth, Jon J., illustrator. II. Kane, Bob, creator.
III. Title.   PZ7.P94967Bat 2016   [E]—dc23   2015026197

10 9 8 7 6 5 4 3 2 1   16 17 18 19 20
Printed in Malaysia 108
First hardcover edition, January 2016

Jon J Muth's artwork was created in watercolor.
Book design by Charles Kreloff and David Saylor

Nothing scares Batman.

Nothing at all, not even the dark. But it's not because he's big and strong.

It's because he knows a secret. A secret he learned long ago, when he was just a little boy named Bruce Wayne . . .

It was a cold night in Gotham City,
but Bruce didn't care. It was movie
night, his favorite night of all.

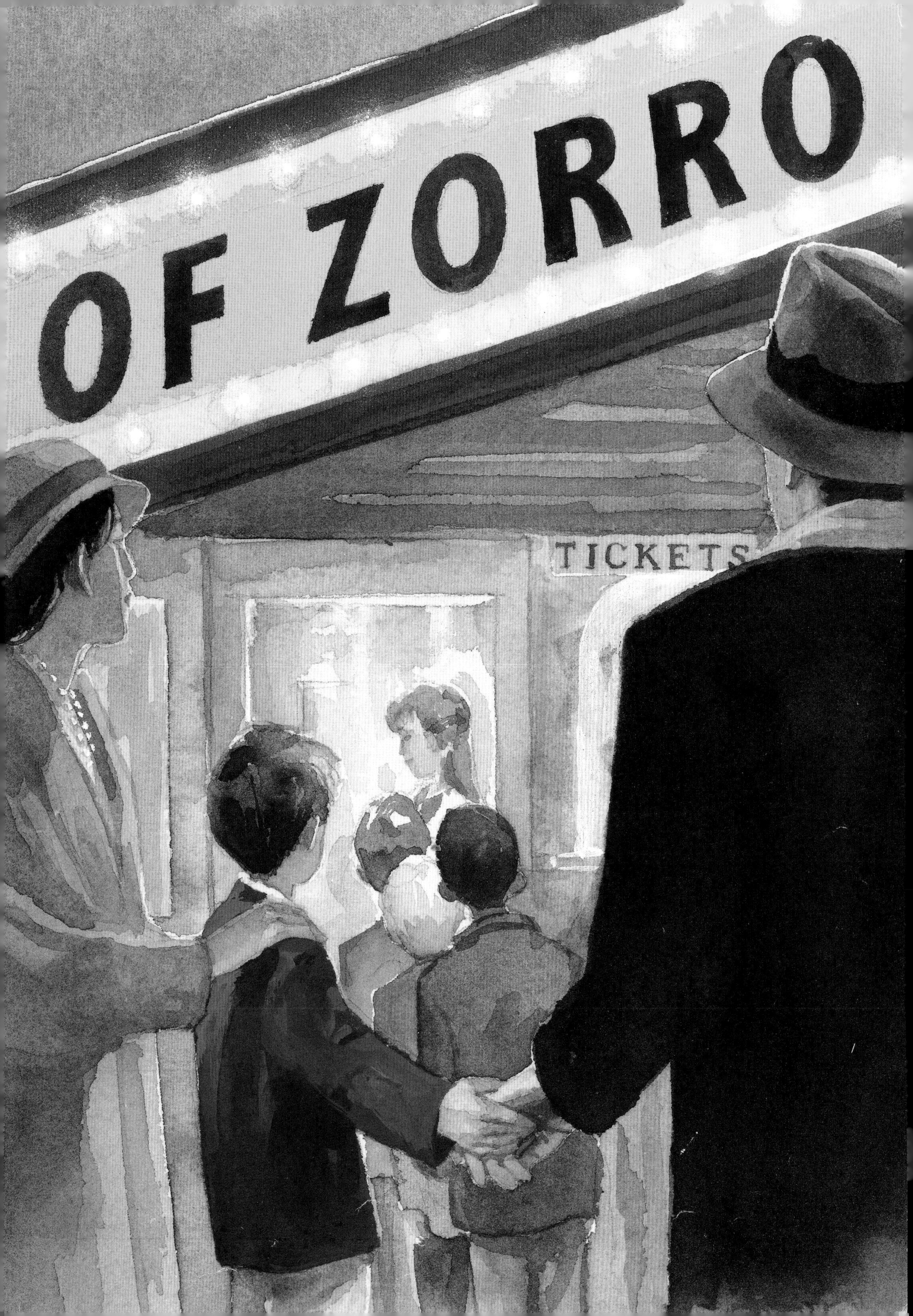
OF ZORRO
TICKETS

The hero had a cape and a mask and a sword.
He fought evil, and he won.

Bruce wanted to be just like him.

Walking home, they came to an alley.
It was pitch black, darker than dark.

But Bruce was young and brave,
and his parents were with him.
He wasn't afraid of the dark.

And when he came out of the dark,
he was alone. His parents were gone!

Bruce lived far outside the city in a
very big house. It looked even bigger now.

Alfred was the butler. He took care of Bruce.
When Bruce complained the house was dark,
Alfred knew what to do.

He put lights in the library. He put lights in the halls. He put lights, lamps, and candles all over the walls.

Bruce wouldn't sleep until the whole house was bright.

"No darkness," he told Alfred. "No darkness," he whispered in his dreams.

Bruce began to take long walks through
the countryside. He'd sit by his favorite tree
for hours, thinking about nothing at all.

One day the sun was extra bright, and Bruce was extra tired. Before he knew it, he'd fallen asleep. And by the time he woke up, it was getting dark.

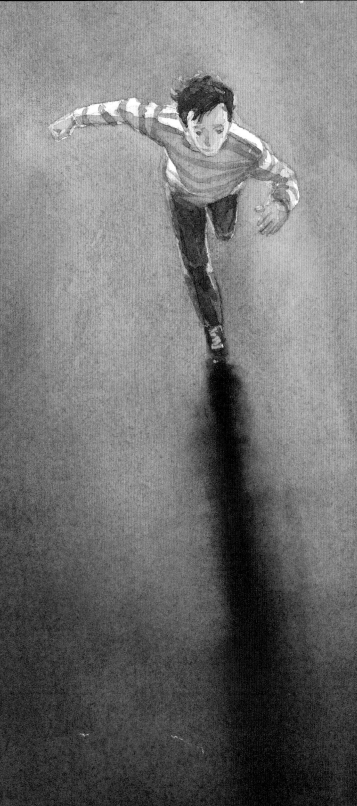

Bruce ran and ran. The sun sank lower.
The sky grew darker. Bruce ran faster.

He didn't see the hole. His foot went in,
then his leg, then him.

He was falling in darkness. Down, down into
the dark, a dark that made the moonlight bright.

WHAM!

He landed hard on cold, wet stone.

His ankle hurt, and he was scared.

Then the darkness came alive. It screeched, it clawed, it swarmed around him. He ran and tripped and fell to the ground.

Slowly, slowly, his eyes adjusted.
The darkness became . . . bats.
Tiny, little bats. Bruce wasn't
afraid of bats.

Then he saw it.

Not a bat. Too big. It was a monster,
and it was coming for him.

Its hot breath fell on his face. The wind from its wings blew back his hair. His fist found a stick and before he could think . . .

The monster . . . backed away.

It was scared . . . of him.

Bruce felt strange, somehow.
Different. Brave.

And he would never be afraid again.